Amelia Bedelia

Makes a Splash

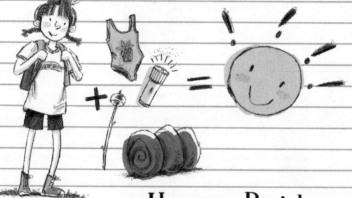

by **Herman Parish**

pictures by **Lynne Avril**

Greenwillow Books
An Imprint of HarperCollins Publishers

Library of Congress Cataloging-in-Publication Data is available.

ISBN 978-0-06-265840-1 (hardback)—ISBN 978-0-06-265839-5 (pbk. ed.)
"Greenwillow Books."

17 18 19 20 21 CG/LSCH 10 9 8 7 6 5 4 3 2 1 First Edition

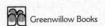

Greenwillow Books

For Ilona & Neil,

a couple of happy campers! —H. P.

For Jeffrey, my inspirator, partner in adventure,

and source of laughter, popcorn, and chocolate—L. A.

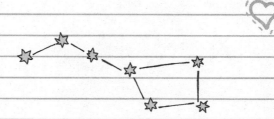

Contents

Chapter 1

Reflections in a Bus Window

Amelia Bedelia had never been so angry. She was mad at her mother and furious with her father. She was even fuming at Finally, her dog. She was most upset with herself, for going along with everything that had led to this

1

moment—her sitting on this bus bound for camp. *Well*, she thought, now she would have four hours to mull over the whole disaster.

Her mother and father and even Finally had come to the parking lot behind the high school to see her off. Other parents were saying good-bye to their daughters, who were climbing aboard, too. But when Amelia Bedelia looked out her window, all she saw was the reflection of her tear-streaked face.

❀ ❀ ❀

Amelia Bedelia knew exactly when this nightmare had begun. It had been just a few weeks ago. It was a glorious day. Spring had, at long last, turned into summer. As she walked home from her after-school dance class, she had been planning what to do with her friends over summer vacation. She vowed to make a list once she got home, so she wouldn't forget anything. She had a lot of fun ideas, and it was going to be a super-great summer! That's when she'd spied smoke billowing behind her house.

"Fire!" hollered Amelia Bedelia, racing up her driveway. She grabbed her mother's garden hose and turned on the

What to do this summer

① ② ③ ④

water. As she rounded the corner of the house, she closed her eyes and squeezed the trigger of the hose sprayer, soaking the plants near the patio.

"Welcome home, sweetheart," said her father. He was standing behind the grill, hidden by thick clouds of smoke, trying to light the charcoal. Amelia Bedelia dropped the hose. A dribble of water splashed onto the patio.

"Good thinking," he said. "Those flowers need a drink."

"Um, okay, Dad," said Amelia Bedelia, relieved she hadn't soaked her father.

When Amelia Bedelia walked into her house, she took a big whiff. Something smelled great! She followed the aroma into the kitchen.

"Yum!" she said to her mother. "What's that?"

"Twice-baked potatoes," said her mother.

"Did you goof them up the first time?" asked Amelia Bedelia.

"Thanks for that vote of confidence," said her mother. She explained the recipe

5

while Amelia Bedelia got a glass of juice
and sat down at the table to make her list
of awesome summer plans before
she forgot them.

Amelia Bedelia looked up a while later
when her father brought a juicy steak,
sizzling from the grill, into the kitchen.

"Looks perfect, honey," said Amelia Bedelia's mother.

Amelia Bedelia and her parents sat down, said grace, and dug in.

"Yum!" said Amelia Bedelia. She noticed that her mom and dad were arching their eyebrows at each other, in the secret language of parents, signaling that an important topic was about to be introduced. Amelia Bedelia wished her chair had a seat belt.

"I got some sad news today," said Amelia Bedelia's mother. "The camp I went to every summer when I was growing up is getting ready to close."

"Ho, ho, ho!" said Amelia Bedelia's

father with a chuckle. "Did summer get canceled?"

Amelia Bedelia hoped he was kidding. She had summer plans. Lots of them.

"Very funny, honey," said her mother. "The camp director, the heart and soul of the place, is closing the camp and retiring."

"That's sad," said Amelia Bedelia. "Isn't that the place where all those funny stories you told us about happened?"

"Yup. Camp Echo Woods," said

9

Amelia Bedelia's mother. "Where my fondest memories were made. I still dream about it sometimes. We were planning to send you one summer." She looked straight at Amelia Bedelia's father and arched one eyebrow.

Uh-oh, thought Amelia Bedelia.

"Amel—" said Amelia Bedelia's father.

"Gee!" interrupted Amelia Bedelia. "It's too bad it's closing before I can go."

"Well, you're in luck," said her father.

"I called today," said her mother. "They had a cancellation, so I snagged that spot for you."

A numb feeling came creeping up

Amelia Bedelia's spine when she realized that her father's joke had come true. Summer, *her* summer, with all her friends and plans and adventures, had just been canceled.

Chapter 2

Sleep Far Away Camp

Amelia Bedelia sprang up from the dining-room table and returned waving her list. "Look! I was planning my summer right here, see?" she said, handing her father the paper. "I don't need help! I have a lot of ideas!"

"I only have one idea," said her father. "Put 'Go to Camp'

12

at the top of your list."

Amelia Bedelia was quick at sizing up a situation. Since it was two against one, she decided to bargain. "How about I go during the day and do what I want when I get home?" she said.

"It's a sleepaway camp, cupcake," said her mother. "Remember?"

Amelia Bedelia studied her list. "I could maybe spare a week," she offered.

"How about eight weeks?" said her father.

8!!!

"What?" wailed Amelia Bedelia. She did some quick multiplication. "One week equals seven days, times eight weeks . . . fifty-six days! I'll go next summer, I promise!"

what??? what??? hat??? what???

13

1 week = 7 days X 8 weeks = 56 days!!!

"There is no next summer," said her father.

"Camp Echo Woods is closing," said her mother.

"Does that mean it's not fun anymore?" said Amelia Bedelia.

"It's a bit primitive for today's kids," said her mother, smiling. "But fun!"

"Like caveman days?" asked Amelia Bedelia.

"Of course not, silly," said her mother. "But the camp was pretty rustic in my day."

"How can a rusty camp be pretty?" said Amelia Bedelia.

"Rustic, not rusty," said Amelia Bedelia's father. "They've got indoor bathrooms now, right, honey?"

"What did they do before that?" Amelia Bedelia asked, her eyes wide.

"Simple!" said her father. "An out-house. Why, when I was a boy . . ."

Amelia Bedelia's head was spinning.

"Never mind," said her mother. "Camp Echo Woods is wonderful. I can tell you that if I hadn't gone there, I wouldn't be who I am today."

Amelia Bedelia was speechless. And whenever she found herself in that situation, she always asked a question.

"You wouldn't be who you are?" she asked.

"That's right," said her mother, nodding.

"Then who would you be?" asked Amelia Bedelia.

"Good question," said Amelia Bedelia's father, his eyes twinkling. "So, honey, who *would* you be?"

Amelia Bedelia's mother glared at him.

Amelia Bedelia's father froze like a deer in headlights and began blinking.

"Can we have dessert now?" asked Amelia Bedelia.

"Great idea!" he said, jumping

up and heading to the kitchen.
"I just bought some rocky
road ice cream!" He dashed
to the kitchen with Finally
barking excitedly at his
heels.

Amelia Bedelia and her mother sat
together at the table. They were both
staring down at their plates. At last Amelia
Bedelia's mother looked up and said, "I can
tell you exactly who I am, right now. I am
the mother of a wonderful daughter. And
I wouldn't trade my life for anything. Of
course, we won't always see eye to eye."

"No, you're taller than I am," said
Amelia Bedelia.

Her mother smiled, took a sip of water,

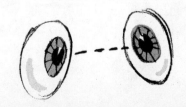

and said, "Your father and I are trying our best to give you the love and the support you need to become the best person you can be. Sometimes the best thing can be getting away from home for a while. Going off to a new place, doing different things with people you've never met before and may not meet again. You can stand back and see yourself. Start figuring out who you are and who you'd like to be."

"Does it have to take eight weeks?" said Amelia Bedelia.

"Actually, it takes the rest of your life," said her mother. "But I understand that eight weeks seems like a long time."

"It's my whole summer," said Amelia Bedelia. "I've been waiting for it all year. I have plans with my friends. Now they'll have fun without me." She started to sob. "Just because camp was great for you doesn't mean it'll be great for me. I don't want to go!"

"Tell you what, sweetie," said Amelia Bedelia's mother. "Your father and I will come visit after four weeks and see how you're doing. If you don't like it, you can come home. Four weeks is the halfway point. Can you meet me halfway?"

Amelia Bedelia got up and walked halfway around the table. Her mother met her there. Opening her arms wide, her mother said, "I love you this much." They hugged for a long, long time.

They were still hugging when Amelia Bedelia's father returned with three bowls of ice cream. "Hey, can I get in on this family hug?" he asked. Amelia Bedelia and her mother laughed and opened their arms to include him, too.

"We're missing Finally," said Amelia Bedelia. "Where is she?"

"Outside," said her father.

Amelia Bedelia went into the backyard. She found Finally by the garden, with a chew toy shaped like a duck. Amelia Bedelia bent down to scratch her behind her ears, but when she did, Finally grabbed her duck and pranced proudly across the yard.

"It's okay, girl. I won't take Mr. Quack," said Amelia Bedelia. "Or do you want me to go away, too?"

Finally wagged her tail.

"Was that a yes or a no?" said Amelia Bedelia.

Finally was so much a member of their family that Amelia Bedelia often forgot that she was a dog. She knew that Finally had run from her out of instinct, to guard her toy. It was like her habit of spinning around and around before she got settled, as if flattening grass into a cozy nest. All dogs have done the same things for thousands of years.

Amelia Bedelia wondered if she had instincts, too. Maybe she should have growled at her parents when they told her about Camp Echo Woods.

"Grrrrrrrrr!" said Amelia Bedelia.

"*Woof!*" answered Finally.

Chapter 3

Homesick Meets Home Sick

When school let out for the summer, Amelia Bedelia only had one week before camp started. The time went by in a blur of shopping for the items she needed on the Camp Echo Woods checklist. Soon, it was her last night at home. Amelia Bedelia's parents helped her pack. They had a system. Her

CAMP CHECKLIST
- Bathing suits
- Bug Spray
- Flashlight
- Cash for store
- Back pack
- Sun hat
- Sunscreen

father read the checklist, calling out items one by one and putting a check mark next to it when Amelia Bedelia located the item and handed it to her mother to pack.

"Bathing suits?" said her father.

"Check," said Amelia Bedelia.

"Bug spray?" said her father.

"Check," said Amelia Bedelia.

"Flashlight?" said her father.

"Check," said Amelia Bedelia.

"Double-check it," said her father.

"You've got the list, make two check marks," said Amelia Bedelia.

"Check that it *works*," he said. "Are the batteries good? You don't want to wind up in the dark. Here, give it to me." He turned it on and turned off the overhead light. He held the flashlight under his chin, pointing it up toward his face. Amelia Bedelia jumped, even though she knew it was her father.

"*Mmmmm-bwah-hah-hah!*" he said, trying to sound scary. "Let me tell you the story about the lost camper who—"

"Honey, it's late," said her mother,

Mmmmm-BWah-hah-hah!!!

turning the light back on. "Amelia Bedelia needs her sleep. Tomorrow is a big day."

The day was hot and humid. Amelia Bedelia was sad and mad. She was also tired, because she hadn't been able to sleep all night. When the driver of the Camp Echo Woods bus started the engine, the air conditioning fogged up the windows immediately.

Amelia Bedelia moved her hand back and forth across the glass like a windshield

wiper, clearing away the condensation to get a last glimpse of her family. Her parents were standing right below her window, with Finally in her father's arms. To them, it looked like she was waving good-bye. They began waving back wildly. Her father waved Finally's paw.

Amelia Bedelia saw her mother wipe away tears. Then the bus lurched forward, with a loud *honk-HONNNNK* good-bye. Finally let out a heartbreaking howl that rang in Amelia Bedelia's ears for miles.

Amelia Bedelia watched the houses,

people, and trees rush by. She would not see any of this again—her family or friends or town—for fifty-six days. Well, twenty-eight. She focused on her face reflected in the window. She looked as miserable and lonely as she felt.

Amelia Bedelia was sitting by herself. The other girls all seemed to know one

another. They'd probably gone to Camp Echo Woods together forever! They looked friendly, but no one talked to her. They were too busy telling stories, laughing, and looking at photos.

They were all wearing the camp uniform—a white shirt, dark blue shorts, and sneakers so new, so blindingly white, that Amelia Bedelia thought they must glow in the dark. She herself was wearing high-top canvas tennis shoes, a green one on her right foot and a red one on her left. As she had climbed aboard the bus, a girl had called out, "Love your shoes! Red and green? Are you one of Santa's elves?" The girls around her had all laughed.

Amelia Bedelia was wearing jeans

and her favorite T-shirt. That morning, she had said to her mother, "I'm looking normal for as long as I can." Her mother had sighed and put a camp uniform on the very top of her stuff so that she could find it easily when she arrived at Camp Echo Woods. Amelia Bedelia figured that her jeans and T-shirt would come in handy if she decided to run away and go back home. After all, if two dogs and a cat could do it, so could she. She'd always been good at incredible journeys.

Yippee!!

At the very edge of town, a car raced up alongside the bus, honking its horn and flashing its lights until the bus driver pulled over and stopped. Amelia Bedelia's heart soared even though she didn't recognize the car. Her parents had come to their senses and had sent someone to rescue her!

But when the bus door opened, she could hear arguing and crying. This was clearly not a rescue operation! Finally the bus driver closed the door again, and a very tall girl with long blond hair walked down the aisle. She sat in the first open seat, right next to Amelia Bedelia.

"Is this seat taken?" asked the girl. Her eyes were red.

"Yes, now it is," said Amelia Bedelia.

"Can I sit here?" asked the girl.

"You already are," said Amelia Bedelia.

"I'm Alice," said the girl, shrugging and holding out her hand.

"I'm Amelia Bedelia," said Amelia Bedelia, shaking Alice's hand.

Alice was staring at Amelia Bedelia's shoes. Amelia Bedelia braced herself for

left side "port" RED

right side "starboard" GREEN

another elf joke.

"Do you sail?" asked Alice.

"I can sail," said Amelia Bedelia.

"I figured," said Alice. "Your sneakers match the running lights on a boat. Your right foot, the starboard foot, is green, and your left foot is red for port."

Amelia Bedelia laughed. What a relief! Now she felt lucky that no one else had taken the seat next to her. What were the chances of meeting a friend right from the start? And Alice had almost missed the bus!

"Are you homesick?" asked Alice, looking intently at Amelia Bedelia's eyes. Anyone could see that Amelia Bedelia had been crying.

Amelia Bedelia was afraid that her voice would break if she tried talking, so she nodded.

"Me too," said Alice. "I'm totally sick of home."

Amelia Bedelia wasn't sure what to say to that. "Have you been to Camp Echo Woods before?" she asked.

"Nope. Have you?" asked Alice.

Amelia Bedelia shook her head and reclined her seat. She soon discovered that she didn't have to talk much. Alice kept talking and talking. Talking about

her parents. Talking about her pets. Talking about her family, including the weird uncle from Pittsburgh who made a million dollars, lost it, then made it back again.

As fascinating as these stories were, Amelia Bedelia was struggling to keep her eyes open. Alice's voice, and the chatter of the other girls, and the droning of the bus engine blended together into a sound very much like the sound she heard when she held her favorite seashell to her ear. It was very relaxing, and Amelia Bedelia fell asleep.

Chapter 4

X You Are Here No KIDDING

Amelia Bedelia woke with a start. The bus had stopped. She looked out the window. They were surrounded by huge pine trees, and the sky above was a deep blue.

"That was no cat nap!" said Alice, putting on her backpack. "You slept for like four hours!"

"Sorry," said Amelia Bedelia. She

looked around the bus. All the girls were gathering up their things.

"I'm sorry I'm so boring," said Alice.

"You are not at all"—Amelia Bedelia yawned—"boring."

Alice rolled her eyes and handed Amelia Bedelia her backpack. "Do you know that you talk in your sleep?" she asked. "Who's Finally?"

"My dog," said Amelia Bedelia. "She's the sweetest, and I miss her so much!"

"I love dogs," Alice agreed.

Amelia Bedelia followed Alice off the bus. The first thing she noticed was a giant trash can. It was a metal drumlike can

without a top. Someone had painted great big daisies all over it. Next to the trash can was a huge painted map of the camp, showing all the buildings and geographical features, such as a hill, a lake, and the woods. The cabins were arranged in clusters. An X marked the spot where they stood.

"Amelia Bedelia, you are here," said Alice, tapping the X.

"Don't remind me," said Amelia Bedelia. She looked at her feet expecting to see a giant X under her red and green sneakers.

"That big place on the hill must be the dining hall," said Alice, pointing to a large building on the map.

"We eat in a hallway?" asked Amelia

Bedelia. "Standing up?"

"I think it's just a giant room with tables and a kitchen," said Alice. "My mom said the food here isn't half bad."

"So it's half good?" asked Amelia Bedelia.

half empty? → half full? You decide!

Alice shrugged. "That's optimistic."

Next to the map was a signpost, and all the signs for various places (ARCHERY and POTTERY and WATERFRONT and LAUNDRY

Counselors' Cabins

Campfire Crescent

Pottery

Arts and Crafts

Campers' Cabins

canoes and boats

Beach

High dive

ECHO

and SHOWERS) were on arrows pointing in different directions. Front and center stood a tall, thin pole, painted white, with a flag snapping in the breeze at the top. The place was beginning to make sense to Amelia Bedelia. She twirled around and around like a ballerina, taking it all in.

But now Amelia Bedelia was getting dizzy. She staggered back and tripped. Just before she hit the ground, a pair of strong hands caught her.

"Whoa there," said the young woman holding her up.

"Nice catch," said Alice.

"Thanks!" said Amelia Bedelia. She was looking at the young woman upside down, but she could tell she was nice.

"Upsy-daisy," said the woman, lifting Amelia Bedelia back to her feet.

"Hey there!" the young woman said. "My name is Peggy."

Amelia Bedelia read the name embroidered on the young woman's shirt. "Thanks, Peggy. Did you borrow

that shirt from Margaret?" she asked.

"Peggy is short for Margaret," said Peggy, smiling. "Who are you?"

"Amelia Bedelia. My name isn't short for anything."

Peggy took a clipboard from under her arm and scanned a list of names. "Aha, here you are," she said. "Bedelia, Amelia."

44

"Nope. That's backward," said Amelia Bedelia. "Amelia comes first. Then Bedelia."

"My list is alphabetical," said Peggy.

"In the alphabet, A comes before B," said Amelia Bedelia.

"Right," said Peggy. "But on my list, last names come first."

So far, Camp Echo Woods was a roller coaster! She had only been here for five minutes, and she was already feeling completely confused. How was she going to last for twenty-eight days?

Alice looked over Peggy's shoulder and pointed at her own name. "Here I am," she said.

"Hi, Alice!" said Peggy. "There are five of you who have never been to Camp

Echo Woods before. We thought it would be a good idea to put all of you newbies in the same cabin with your own counselor. That's me!" Peggy smiled. "Let's grab your bags and get you settled in. The others are already here. Follow me!"

Peggy nodded toward the large house facing the lake. "That's where Mrs. Evans lives," she said. "This is her camp."

Just then, as though she had been summoned by the mention of her name, a lady with a walking stick appeared on the porch and called out, "Peggy, who do we have here?"

Peggy steered Amelia Bedelia and Alice over to the porch and introduced them.

Amelia Bedelia thought that Mrs. Evans looked older than a fossil, but her voice was clear and strong.

"Amelia Bedelia?" said Mrs. Evans. "Sounds familiar."

"My mother went here when she was a girl," said Amelia Bedelia.

"Ah, yes, I remember," said Mrs. Evans. "And she called me to see if you could join us this summer. Did she drive you here?"

"She sure did," said Amelia Bedelia.

"I didn't want to come. This was all her idea."

Mrs. Evans frowned and thumped her stick on the porch. *Thump. Thump.* THUMP THUMP

"Actually, Amelia Bedelia and Alice came by bus," said Peggy quickly.

"Well, that's neither here nor there," said Mrs. Evans.

"Then where is it?" asked Amelia Bedelia.

"Where's what?" asked Mrs. Evans.

"Where's that?" said Amelia Bedelia. "If that's not there, then where is it? Is it here, like on the big map?"

Mrs. Evans looked at Peggy, who smiled and shrugged.

"I'm just happy they both got here," Peggy said. "And that's that."

"I'll be happier to see you in uniform, Amelia Bedelia," said Mrs. Evans.

"I'm taking them to their cabin," said Peggy. "Amelia Bedelia will change, and we'll be back for your greeting to the campers. Let's go, girls. Follow me!"

Chapter 5

Star Struck

Based on the map, Amelia Bedelia had guessed that the sleeping cabins were pretty close to Mrs. Evans's house. But the hike was long, and when they finally arrived, Amelia Bedelia was worn out.

This made her think that the map was not all that accurate.

Peggy headed to the far cabin and said, "Here you are. Home sweet home for the next two months!"

Here, thought Amelia Bedelia, *for two months*. She didn't want to be here. Here was camp. She wanted to be there, back home. Panic surged through her. She was still wearing street clothes. If she started running right now . . .

"Polaris? Who's Polaris?" asked Alice, tracing the letters carved into a wooden plaque next to the door.

"Every cabin is named for a star," said Peggy.

"I've never heard of

Polaris," said Amelia Bedelia. "Is Polaris a movie star? A rock star?"

"A TV star?" asked Alice.

"Polaris is a real star," said Peggy. "I'll introduce you one night."

"I've never met a real star," said Amelia Bedelia. Despite herself, she was intrigued. Maybe there was hope for Camp Echo Woods.

Just then, laughter burst out inside the cabin. It got louder when Peggy swung the door open and led them in. "Amelia Bedelia and Alice," she said, "meet your fellow campers."

There was a big tangle of arms and legs and white and blue uniforms on the floor at their feet. The tangle stopped rolling around but kept on giggling.

"One, two . . . three heads," said Alice.

The pile turned into three separate girls, who got to their feet slowly, each carefully keeping at least one hand on the most beat-up teddy bear Amelia Bedelia had ever seen.

"You ladies look like puppies wrestling over a chew toy," said Peggy. "I'd like you to meet Alice."

Alice took a small step forward and waved.

"And this is Bedelia Amelia," said Peggy, putting a hand on her shoulder.

Amelia Bedelia's eyes grew wide. Snapping her head around, she stared at Peggy, who smiled and winked. "Sorry, I just had to see the look on your face."

"She means *Amelia* Bedelia," said Amelia Bedelia to the others.

Peggy pointed at the other campers. "Meet Amy, Nannette, and Lisha," she said.

"A-nnette," said Annette.

"A-lisha," said Alisha. "You forgot the As."

"Sorry," said Peggy. "I'm still learning your names."

A A A A A A

"All our first names start with A," said Amelia Bedelia.

"Hey, that's right," said Peggy. "You're Straight As."

The girls looked at one another and nodded. They felt just like they'd been admitted to a secret club.

"It's cool, but it's pretty weird," said Amy.

"That's life," said Alisha.

Amy Alisha Amelia Bedelia Alice Annette

C'est la vie!

"*C'est la vie*," said Annette.

"That's French," whispered Alice to Amelia Bedelia. "*C'est la vie.*" Looking over at Annette, she said, "You're not from around here."

"I'm from Paris," said Annette. "My mother grew up in America. She spent every summer here at—"

Peggy blew her whistle. "Ladies. Ladies. Ladies," she said, clapping her hands after each word. "You'll have hours and hours to get to know one another. Now it's time for the opening ceremony. Follow me!"

Peggy took the lead, setting a brisk pace for about five seconds. Suddenly she stopped, so abruptly that the girls ran into one another like dominoes.

56

"Whoa, whoa, whoa!" said Peggy. She held up both hands and began walking down the line of campers, halting when she came to Amelia Bedelia. "What's wrong with this picture?" she asked.

"What picture?" said Amelia Bedelia.

Peggy smiled and said, "You need to put the 'you' into uniform."

Oh no! Her camp uniform! "I'll go change," said Amelia Bedelia.

"No time," said Peggy. "Grab it and bring it with you. You can change when we get there."

Amelia Bedelia had turned to walk back to the cabin when Peggy blew her whistle.

"Run! Run! Run!" called Peggy, clapping after each word.

Amelia Bedelia raced to the cabin and grabbed a uniform. Clutching it under her arm, Amelia Bedelia sprinted back to the group. The Straight As cheered.

"Atta girl!" yelled Peggy. "We'll get there on time if we jog."

Everyone had already gathered around the flagpole. Peggy picked out a spot in the ring of campers for the Polaris cabin to stand. "We'll gather right here before breakfast, lunch, and dinner," she said. "So if there are any announcements or schedule changes or if someone sees Bigfoot, we'll know right away."

"Who has big feet?" asked Alisha.

58

"Mrs. Evans," said Annette. "*Enorme!* My mom says she laughs about it herself."

Amy said, "I bet they stink, too."

"Uh-uh-uh," said Peggy. "No camper is allowed to say anything bad or mean about another camper. That goes for Mrs. Evans, too, and all the counselors." Then she clapped three times and said, "Mrs. Evans will be here any second, Amelia Bedelia. Put on your uniform."

"Where?" said Amelia Bedelia.

"Right here," said Peggy, pointing at the ground.

"In the middle of camp?" said Amelia Bedelia. "Right now?"

"It's just us," said Alice. "Hurry!"

"Out in the open?" said Amelia Bedelia.

"We'll shield you," said Alisha. She and the three other girls gathered around Amelia Bedelia, their backs to her, their arms interlocked.

"Excellent teamwork!" said Peggy.

Amelia Bedelia was taking off her jeans when she heard some shocking news.

"Here come the guys from the cabin next door," said Alisha.

"Guys? Are you kidding?" said Amelia Bedelia, hopping around in her bare feet and quickly pulling on her shorts. "I thought this camp was for girls only!"

"I've only met Sam and Alex," said Amy.

Amelia Bedelia couldn't see any guys, and she hoped that they couldn't see her, either. She took off her T-shirt.

"Chris is nice," said Annette.

Amelia Bedelia struggled into her camp shirt. She got her arms through the sleeves, but her head was stuck. She turned around and around in a circle. She felt like Finally.

"Hi, Danni. Hi, Toni," said Alisha.

"Danny and Tony!" yelled Amelia Bedelia. "Are you serious?"

"No, we're Polaris," said Annette. "They're Sirius."

Amelia Bedelia stumbled over someone's foot and down she went, taking the girls of Polaris with her.

The good thing was that her head popped through the neck of her shirt. The bad thing was that now she could see Mrs. Evans striding straight toward her.

Chapter 6

"Are We Still on Earth?"

Mrs. Evans stood in front of the fallen cluster of Polaris girls. Peggy untangled them one by one, giving each girl a hand up, until Amelia Bedelia was revealed at the center of the pile. Mrs. Evans shook her head and said, "How can anyone get so filthy so fast? At least you've got your uniform on, Amelia Bedelia. You're a mess, but I can tell that you're our mess."

Mrs. Evans continued on to the flagpole. She was carrying a staff with a notch at the top in the shape of the letter V. She raised the staff high in the air. The counselors stopped talking to their campers and each raised one hand, making a letter V with their first two fingers. The campers quickly grew quiet, too, and made the same sign with their raised hands. Amelia Bedelia and the

other Polaris girls, who were trying not to giggle, shrugged and copied them. When it was totally, eerily quiet, Mrs. Evans began to speak.

"Heavens to Murgatroyd, here we are for another summer at Echo Woods. Welcome back, ladies, and welcome to our five new campers. Now that your kit and caboodle is stowed, Counselor Peggy will show you the whole shebang. Just don't expect to be mollycoddled or live the life of Riley. Nothing namby-pamby lasts very long out here in the boondocks.

"Our cook is making grub that will stick to your ribs. We have a wonderful nurse, should anyone come down

grub

blah kit and caboodle blah blah whole shebang blah blah mollycoddled blah Life blah blah blah of Riley blah namby pamby blah grub blah boondocks blah blah whim whams blah blah blah collywobbles blah blah blah heebie-jeebies blah blah blah flies in the ointment blah

65

with the whim-whams, a case of the collywobbles, or just the heebie-jeebies. There won't be any flies in the ointment.

"About the only thing that bugs me is a litterbug. That's when I see red. Now you know how I feel, so we won't shilly-shally another second. Let's seize this summer. Onward!"

Mrs. Evans waved her staff above her head in triumph. The counselors cheered. The campers whooped. As Mrs. Evans led everyone toward the dining hall, the Polaris girls stood frozen, looking at one another with utter bewilderment.

"What did she just say?" asked Alisha.

"Am I still in the United States?" asked Annette.

"Am I still on Earth?" added Amy.

Even Alice was shaking her head.

Truthfully Amelia Bedelia felt relieved. For once she wasn't the only one who didn't have a clue what someone was talking about.

"Mrs. Evans is from another era," said Peggy.

"Yeah, the Jurassic period," said Amy.

Alisha laughed. "When she was our age, I bet she had a pet dinosaur."

"Remember the rule I told you about." Peggy smiled. "Trust me. You'll grow to love her. We all do. Now, let's go eat."

"Must I eat a grub?" asked Annette.

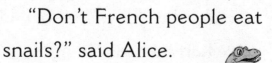

snails
escargot

"Don't French people eat snails?" said Alice.

"Not me," said Annette.

"Lunchtime!" Peggy called out, clapping three times. "I'll translate what Mrs. Evans said while we eat. Once you get past the language barrier, she has tons of experience in the outdoors."

The dining hall was a big room filled with tables and chairs. It was crowded and noisy. The Polaris table was next to the Sirius table. "Girls of Polaris," said Peggy, "meet your neighbors, Sirius. You are the North Star, they are the Dog Star. Their cabin is next to yours."

As they introduced themselves, Amelia Bedelia realized that these girls were actually the "boys" who had surprised her when she was changing.

"Hi, I'm Christine. But you can call me Chris," said Chris.

"I'm Danni, short for Daniela, and this is my friend Antonia," said Danni.

"Toni," said Antonia.

Sam and Alex turned out to be Samantha and Alexandra. They smiled at Amelia Bedelia, and she smiled back—until she realized where she had seen them before. These were the girls who had laughed at her red and green sneakers on the bus!

After lunch, the Polaris girls went back to the cabin and put on their bathing suits. Peggy gave them a quick tour of the camp, so they'd know where the showers,

toilets, and laundry were located and where the counselors slept.

"That's my cabin," said Peggy, "in case you need me in an emergency." She pointed at a two-foot-tall statue of a garden gnome wearing a backpack. "And that's my boyfriend standing guard."

As she led them past the campfire crescent, Peggy said, "We have a campfire twice a week, with lots of singing, some goofy skits, snacks, and stories."

"Ghost stories?" asked Amy. "Like the one about the lost camper who—"

"No! The last thing we need is a camp full of kids so afraid of the dark they can't go to sleep."

They toured the arts and crafts buildings, dropped by the canoes and rowboats, and then headed to the beach.

"Okay, Polaris! Time to make a splash," said Peggy.

The Straight As stood on the coarse sand, ready to dive in.

"On your mark, get set—"

TWEET! Peggy blew her whistle, and the girls dashed into the water. In less than three seconds, they were all shrieking.

"AHHHHHHHHHHHHHH!!!!!!!!!!!"

"It's freezing!" screamed Alisha.

Amelia Bedelia couldn't even speak. The lake was so cold that her teeth chattered—and her body shook all on its own, as if it belonged to someone else.

Brrrr!

"Echo Lake is deep and cold," said Michelle, the lifeguard. She laughed. "Don't worry! It'll warm up by next month. So don't get cold feet!"

Cold feet? Amelia Bedelia had cold *everything*. Still, she felt a pang of disappointment. She'd be back home when the lake was warm. Michelle called them out of the water to warm up, and she explained how the buddy system worked, so they could swim safely. Then it was back into the lake to see how well they could swim and tread water. Annette was the fastest, swimming like a little seal.

"You'll go swimming every morning and afternoon," said Peggy after they'd dried off and put their uniforms back on. They walked over to the trading post, and then it was time for dinner. Even though the food was half good, Amelia Bedelia almost fell asleep in it. She could not wait to go back to the cabin and climb into her bunk.

"One last thing before lights out," said Peggy. "Please write a note or letter home to let your families know you arrived safely. I'll mail them the old-fashioned way for you. You have plenty to talk about after today, but just a line or two will do the trick!"

Amelia Bedelia was cozy and comfortable in her bunk, and she had no idea what to say to her parents. She was still mad at them. The first thing she saw when she opened her notebook was her

summer vacation to-do list.

She tore it out and set it next to the list she had been given of the daily activities at Camp Echo Woods. Her summer plan had a few amazing and wonderful things to do in one day. Her camp plan had more than twenty things to do each and every day. At the top of the camp schedule she wrote:

Mom and Dad, I wish you were here . . .

At the top of her vacation to-do list, she wrote:

. . . and I was there.

She folded the lists together, slid them into an envelope, wrote her home address on the envelope, and gave it to Peggy.

Once Peggy had all five letters, she

74

said, "I'll put these in the mail and see you in the morning, newbies. Good night! Don't let the bedbugs bite!"

Bedbugs! thought Amelia Bedelia. She'd packed mosquito repellent and stuff for ticks and chiggers. And what about those litterbugs that made Mrs. Evans so angry?

Amelia Bedelia was exhausted, but there was one last thing she had to do. Taking her pen, she made a tiny mark on the wall next to her bunk.

That showed that this day was officially over. One down, twenty-seven to go. That would be halfway, when her parents had promised to meet her and take her back home with them, if she wanted.

 75

Chapter 7

Fire, When Ready

The next morning, Amelia Bedelia was afraid to get out of bed. She had woken up by herself. No alarm clock. No one shaking her awake, worrying that she'd be late. Not even Finally bounding onto her bed. She was awakened by a voice singing so sweetly that she thought that it must be an angel circling outside.

Or the ghost of that lost camper. Amelia Bedelia was scared to look.

Someone beneath her was snoring like a buzz saw. Amelia Bedelia blinked her eyes open and peeked at the bottom bunk. Alice snorted and turned over just as the singer came through the cabin door.

"Good morning, Peggy," whispered Amelia Bedelia, waving a tiny wave. Peggy kept right on singing, never missing a note. She was singing about baby birds waking

up on the day they would fly for the first time.

"Amelia Bedelia, you have a stubborn streak," sang Peggy sweetly. "First we can't get you into your uniform, and now we can't get you out of it."

That's when it dawned on Amelia Bedelia that she'd been so tired last night that she'd slept in her clothes.

After everyone was up and dressed (and Amelia Bedelia had changed), they met Peggy outside.

"Ladies, the day is young and so are you," said Peggy. "We've got lots to do. Let's shake off our sleepies!"

The Straight As formed a circle around Peggy for warm-up stretches.

"Pay attention," she said. "Tomorrow, one of you will lead these exercises."

Once they were limber and awake, they hiked over to the main meeting circle to join the other campers for announcements before breakfast. Mrs. Evans was waving a piece of paper over her head. "Girls, make sure that you keep your schedule of activities handy.

79

That way we can all be on the same page."

Oh, great, thought Amelia Bedelia. *The person in charge is making less sense today than she did yesterday!* How could Mrs. Evans expect all of them to fit on that tiny page? Plus, she'd mailed her schedule home to her parents. Maybe she could share Alice's schedule.

Just then, a gust of wind blew the piece of paper out of Mrs. Evans's hand. It went skittering along the ground. A counselor quickly stepped on it, covering it with her shoe, so it wouldn't blow away.

Amelia Bedelia turned to Alice and whispered, "See, only one person can fit on that page."

"Did Mrs. Evans just litter?" asked Alice.

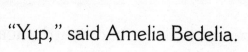

"Yup," said Amelia Bedelia.

After a delicious breakfast of yummy blueberry pancakes and bacon, Peggy led the Polaris girls to their first activity.

"I teach archery in the mornings," said Peggy. "So I'm dropping you off with my friend Melody. She'll teach you how to be outdoorsmen."

"I don't want to be a man," said Annette.

"Me neither," said Alisha.

"I'd rather be an outdoorswoman," said Amy.

"Or an indoorswoman," said Alice.

Amelia Bedelia was beginning to feel right at home.

Peggy began walking backward, facing the girls as she talked. "We've got just enough time to learn a song along the way," she said, launching into the lyrics. She didn't sound like an angel anymore— she was more like one of the girls, as she sang at the top of her lungs.

"Black socks, they never get dirty
The longer you wear 'em, the blacker they get.
Sometimes I think I should wash 'em.
But something keeps telling me
Oh no, not yet, not yet, not yet. . . ."

The Straight As laughed.

"The song can go on and on," said

Peggy. "If you say 'black socks ten,' then everyone has to sing 'not yet' ten times while you count them off."

"Black socks twenty!" yelled Amy.

They'd just sung the last "not yet" when they arrived at a place that looked as if the pioneers had just left in a covered wagon. Peggy introduced them to Melody, then headed off to teach archery.

"Gooood mornin', Polaris! I'm Melody. Welcome to Survival Skills. Today we're going to learn one of the most important skills for surviving in the wilderness, how to build and start a fire."

"I was told never to play with matches," said Amelia Bedelia.

"That's right," said Melody. "We won't

be using matches, and we're not playing. Out in the woods, you may need a fire to signal people to rescue you, to dry out your clothes, to warm you up, to cook your food, even to keep wild animals at bay."

Melody had everyone's attention now.

"I thought this was Echo Lake," said Amelia Bedelia. "Where's the bay?"

"Hold your questions, please! Now, there are two main ways to start a fire safely," said Melody. "One is the tepee method, and the other is the log-cabin method."

Annette raised her hand. "Why are they named after tepees and log cabins?"

"Because that's what they look like,"

said Melody, holding up a big diagram. "Let's build one of each. We need to clear an area, arrange these stones in a circle, then gather some tinder, kindling, and logs."

The girls got to work making the area safe to build their fires. Then they grabbed handfuls of dry grass and moss, some small sticks, and a few larger pieces of wood.

"Remember to leave a little door in your tepee," said Melody.

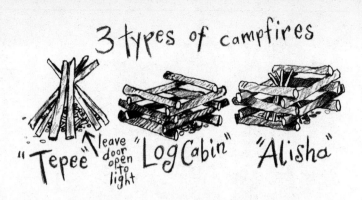

3 types of campfires

"Tepee" — leave door open to light — "Log Cabin" "Alisha"

"You need to light the tinder inside."

"What if you built a tiny tepee fire inside the log cabin?" said Alisha. "That would set the log cabin on fire from the inside."

"Nice idea!" said Melody. "You're thinking out of the box, just like a Camp Echo Woods camper!"

"Now all we need is a match," said Alice, once the Straight As had constructed their tepee and log-cabin structures.

"Here you go," said Melody, handing her a rock. It was light brown with a milky edge, and it looked like a chip from a larger stone.

flint

"That's flint," she said. "It's been used to start fires since the days of the caveman."

"And cavewoman," said Amy.

"Yeah," said Alisha. "They probably had to light fires to cook saber-toothed tigers for dinner."

Melody smiled. "There is evidence that our ancestors as far back as the Stone Age used controlled fire to cook."

Scooping up a handful of tinder, she formed it into something that resembled a little bird's nest, making a depression in the middle with her thumbs.

Taking the flint, she held it over the tinder and struck the edge with a small steel bar. Nothing happened. Melody turned the flint around and tried again. Nothing happened again. The girls looked at one another. Amelia Bedelia was feeling bad for Melody, who turned the flint around *again* and, this time, struck it much harder with the steel. A shower of sparks rained down on the tinder.

"Oooh, baby fireworks," said Annette.

A tiny spark began glowing in the tinder, sending up a curl of smoke. "Blow gently," Melody said to Alice. "Feed more tinder into the glow."

A bigger wisp of smoke rose up until there was a glow inside the tinder and then . . . *poof*! The little ball of tinder became a little ball of flames.

Each Straight A got the chance to

start a fire using flint and steel. They also learned how to extinguish a fire safely and completely. Too soon, Peggy arrived to take them to their next activity.

"Tomorrow we'll learn some basic first aid," said Melody. "Then on to knots!"

"This is way more fun than playing with matches," said Amy. "Not that I would ever do something so stupid and dangerous."

The other girls looked over at Amy.

"Yeah, right," said Alisha.

Chapter 8

ECHO ECHO ECHO

One day after supper, the Polaris girls were hanging out in the dining hall. Outside, there was a huge herb garden that was glowing in the late afternoon light. The garden had been planted  by the cook's husband, Herbert, so everyone called it Herb's garden. It was the secret ingredient that made the

 **90**

food at Camp Echo Woods so delicious.

Amelia Bedelia adored the smell of fresh herbs. She closed her eyes and imagined that she was back home in her mother's garden, snuggling with Finally.

The first campfire of the summer was planned for later, and most of the campers were practicing songs and skits. Their voices blended with the music of the bees in Herb's garden until it felt like the whole camp was buzzing with excitement.

Later, when the sun had finally set and it was time for the campfire, Peggy led them to a spot near the front. They squeezed together so they could all fit on one huge log.

"Tonight you observe, newbies," said

Peggy. "Next time you can do a skit for the camp."

The Straight As sat looking all around. They were on the edge of Echo Lake, facing west. Right in front of them were two log-cabin fires, about four feet tall, ready to be lit.

Alice pointed at the closest one and said, "Hey, Alisha, look!"

"There's a tepee inside!" said Annette. "That was Alisha's idea!"

"Do you think it will work?" asked Alisha.

Once the sun dipped behind the mountain on the other side of the lake, Camp Echo Woods got dark very quickly. A girl with a bugle played taps as the other campers sang the words.

"Day is done, gone the sun . . ."

Amelia Bedelia thought it was the most beautiful song she had ever heard. So simple. Perfect for being in nature.

When the final bugle note had faded across the lake, Melody came forward. She explained that a new camper had suggested an improvement to the camp-fire design, so Mrs. Evans had asked that she light both fires tonight.

"Alisha, please join me!" said Melody.

"The Straight As stick together," whispered Alisha to the other Polaris girls. "Come on!"

The Polaris girls tried not to look at or even think about all the other campers staring at them.

Amelia Bedelia crossed her fingers as Alisha whacked the steel with a piece of flint. A shower of sparks hit the tinder, setting it ablaze in a few seconds. The fire quickly caught, burning brightly into the summer sky.

Melody led the applause as the girls went back to their log.

Now the real fun began. There were songs and skits. Some were pretty goofy, but still funny, and everyone had the giggles in no time.

Both fires popped and crackled. Amelia Bedelia could feel the heat carrying cinders and sparks aloft. She looked up at the little yellow-and-white lights. It was hard to tell which were sparks and which were stars.

At the end of the evening, Melody and Peggy helped everyone make s'mores, and then Mrs. Evans told a story about the early days of the camp, and how it had been hard to get the camp off the ground. Amelia Bedelia munched on her s'more and looked around at the lake, the distant mountain, the softly glowing fire, and her new friends. She was happy that Camp Echo Woods had stayed on this ground right here.

Then Mrs. Evans led them in the anthem of Camp Echo Woods. All the girls stood and put their right hands over their hearts as they sang.

"E's for living enthusiastically.

C is for our camaraderie.

H is for a life in harmony.

O is for our oath we pledge to thee.

Put us all together, we spell

ECHO!" ECHO

They did not sing the word "echo." They shouted or hollered or bellowed or

ECHO ECHO

screamed it. Then they stopped suddenly, listening to the echo, echo, echo, reverberate across the lake. When the sound had faded completely, they sang:

"Resounding in our hearts eternally."

No one made a peep after that. They all went back to their cabins happy and full and went to sleep without saying much of anything. Drifting off, Amelia Bedelia kept imagining sparks floating skyward until she could not tell the difference between them and the stars.

Chapter 9

Vegging Out

One night two weeks later dinner promised to be memorable, and not just because spaghetti and meatballs was by far the most popular meal at Camp Echo Woods. Mrs. Evans was joining the Polaris girls at their table for supper and conversation. One of the Straight As would be acting as the server, so no one—especially Mrs. Evans—would have to jump up to get seconds or water or milk or juice.

"Let's make sure this goes smoothly," said Peggy. "Has anyone been a waitress before?"

When nobody volunteered, Amelia Bedelia slowly raised her hand.

"Great!" said Peggy. "Where did you work?"

"In a diner," said Amelia Bedelia.

"Perfect," said Peggy. "You'll be our server tonight."

It was far from perfect. Amelia Bedelia had been fired from Pete's Diner after

less than an hour on the job, after a truck driver had ordered a piece of pie. He had been in a hurry and had asked her to step on it. So she had. *Splat!*

"Don't worry," said Peggy. "You can do it. Sometimes Mrs. Evans is hard to understand. If you get confused, just signal me. I'll help you."

The Polaris girls arrived in the dining hall ten minutes early, looking shipshape. They had showered, put on clean uniforms, and combed the tangles out of their hair. It wasn't long before Mrs. Evans arrived, too.

"Thank you for inviting me to join you tonight," said Mrs. Evans.

"Our pleasure," said Peggy.

"You don't look familiar," said Mrs. Evans to Amelia Bedelia. "Have we met before?"

"Yes. I'm still Amelia Bedelia," said Amelia Bedelia. "My mother went here a long time ago."

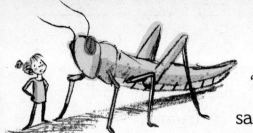

"Now I remember," said Mrs. Evans. "I didn't recognize you all spiffed up. I knew your mother when she was knee-high to a grasshopper."

Amelia Bedelia was stunned. "I don't think she was ever that short," she said as she filled the water glasses. *Do grasshoppers even have knees?* she wondered.

Amelia Bedelia served heaping helpings of spaghetti and meatballs. She inspected every plate before she put it on the table, hoping to spot any half-bad food and exchange it for some that was half good.

"This is our last year of camp at Echo Woods," said Mrs. Evans. "How

I wish my husband, Harold, was here."

"I'll save him a plate," said Amelia Bedelia. "Is he coming soon?"

"Harold is my late husband," said Mrs. Evans.

"How late is he going to be?" asked Amelia Bedelia. "Maybe the kitchen will keep his dinner warm."

"Really *late*, Amelia Bedelia," said Alice. She opened her eyes wide and held

 up her glass. "Juice, please."

As Amelia Bedelia was filling Alice's glass, Peggy whispered so that only Amelia Bedelia could hear. "Her husband expired."

"Expired?" said Amelia Bedelia loudly. "Like milk?"

"Yes, I would," said Amy, holding up her glass.

"Years ago, Harold bought Echo Lake and all the land around it," said Mrs. Evans. "He wanted to share this beautiful spot with future generations, so we built Camp Echo Woods. My Harold was always ahead of his time."

Amelia Bedelia went back to the kitchen confused. If Harold was ahead

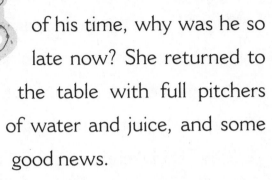

of his time, why was he so late now? She returned to the table with full pitchers of water and juice, and some good news.

"I asked the cook to save a plate for your late husband," she said to Mrs. Evans.

"Pssst . . . Amelia Bedelia," whispered Peggy. "Her husband is no longer with us. He has departed."

"Oh, I'm sorry. I must have just missed him!" said Amelia Bedelia.

"I still miss my Harold," said Mrs. Evans. "Even though I lost him more than twenty years ago."

"Gosh," said Amelia Bedelia. "If he's been lost for that long, he may never get here."

"Amelia Bedelia," said Mrs. Evans. "Do you understand that my husband died?"

"Oh," said Amelia Bedelia. "I'm sorry." She went back to the kitchen to cancel his spaghetti dinner. When she returned, they were still talking about him.

"Did your husband linger long?" asked Peggy.

"No, thank goodness," said Mrs. Evans. "Harold was a great outdoorsman. He didn't want to be a vegetable."

"Me neither," said Amelia Bedelia. "I'd hate to be a carrot. How would you like to be buried up to your forehead in dirt?"

Mrs. Evans laughed loudly.

"Remember the rules," said Peggy. "It's not kind to call a sick person a vegetable."

"But if you had to be a vegetable in a play or for Halloween," said Mrs. Evans, "what vegetable would you hate to be?"

"Cauliflower!" said Amy. "It looks like a brain. Gross!"

brussels sprouts

cauliflower

"Brussels sprouts," said Alisha. "Or cabbage. Yucko!"

string beans

"String beans," said Alice. "Because everyone calls me that because I'm tall."

cabbage

It was Peggy's turn. "Okra," she said. "The stuff that runs out when you cut it

okra

open looks like someone sneezed."

"*Eeeeeewww!*" sang the Straight As, in a chorus.

"Your turn, Mrs. Evans," said Peggy.

Mrs. Evans squinted her eyes and said, "Kohlrabi."

"*Coalwhatee?*" said Amy. "Is that a real vegetable?"

Kohlrabi.

"Kohlrabi looks like a small mutant cabbage from Mars," said Mrs. Evans. "And it tastes worse."

Campers at other tables were turning around to see what all the laughing was about. Amelia Bedelia noticed that when Mrs. Evans was having fun, her wrinkles weren't so noticeable. She seemed younger when she was laughing, not like a fossil at all. The only problem was that now she was laughing so hard she started coughing.

"Would you like something to drink?" asked Amelia Bedelia.

"Yes, thank you," said Mrs. Evans, raising her glass. "Would you give me a splash of juice?"

So that was exactly what Amelia Bedelia did.

Chapter 10

Pollution: Heavy or Light?

The next night the Polaris girls stopped by Mrs. Evans's house so Amelia Bedelia could leave a note on her door apologizing for the juice bath. Amelia Bedelia still felt terrible about it. She was hoping that the night hike would take her mind off it.

The landscape was mysterious and

dim, lit by a tiny crescent moon. They followed Peggy down a road that soon turned into a trail and then became a narrow winding path through the trees.

"Lucky us," said Peggy. "When the moon sets . . ."

"Why do we need blankets?" asked Alice. "Are we spending the night out here?"

"We're just going to veg out for a while," said Peggy.

Everyone laughed. *Oh no, not more vegetables!*

"Actually," said Peggy, "we've got a date with the Milky Way."

"Yum!" said Amelia Bedelia.

The moon was beginning to set when

they came to a big clearing covered in grass and clover. Peggy spread out her blanket, then plopped down on her back. Everyone copied her, including Amelia Bedelia, who turned around and around, flattening the grass before spreading out her blanket and lying down on it.

She felt just like Finally, circling around before lying down, even on the rug. Now Amelia Bedelia was sure that she must have animal instincts herself! She barked, and the other girls started howling at the moon, too.

When the moon had finally set and everyone had stopped giggling, they couldn't see Peggy or one another.

"It's so dark," said Annette.

"Dark with a capital D," added Amy.

"At least the stars are getting brighter," said Alice.

"No, they're the same," said Peggy. "They just seem brighter because there is no light pollution."

"There's no heavy pollution, either," said Amelia Bedelia.

"Light pollution is caused by the light in our homes and cities— like lights from office buildings, shopping malls, and streetlamps," said Peggy. "Out here at Camp Echo Woods there is much less light pollution."

"Is that smoke?" asked Alisha, pointing overhead.

"Or maybe fog?" asked Alice. "Or mist?"

"That?" asked Peggy, turning on her flashlight and pointing it at a speckled band of light stretching across the sky.

"Are those stars?" asked Amelia Bedelia.

you are here

"Meet the Milky Way, our galaxy," said Peggy. "The Milky Way contains our solar system. We're looking at its edge. It circles around to the other side of the earth too, where it's daytime."

Peggy pointed her light straight up.

"There are hundreds of billions of stars up there. Trillions of planets."

"Scary!" said Amy.

"I like that," said Amelia Bedelia. "Maybe a bunch of friends are up there, pointing a flashlight at us, wondering who we are."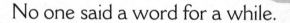

No one said a word for a while.

"Look!" said Peggy, wiggling her light on a star. "That's Polaris, the North Star. It stays almost motionless all year. If you know where north is, you can find south, east, and . . ."

"What was that?" shouted Alisha, pointing at a thin white streak fading overhead.

"A shooting star," said Peggy. "Those happen all the time, at night and during the day. Only now, out here, you can actually see them."

"*Très jolie*," said Annette.

"Polaris is easy to find," said Peggy. "See those stars shaped like a dipper, like for scooping water? That's the Big Dipper. It points to the handle of the Little Dipper. That star at the handle's tip, the brightest, is Polaris, the North Star."

"Are we brighter than Sirius?" asked Alisha.

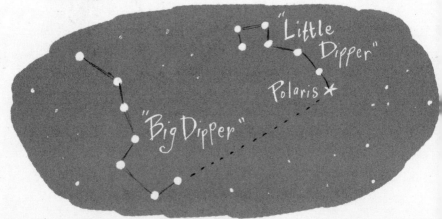

Sirius

"Canis Major"

"Nope," said Peggy. "Sirius is the brightest star in the sky. We can't see it here at night until fall or winter. It's called the Dog Star, in the constellation Canis Major, which stands for 'big dog.' Long ago, people started seeing groups of stars as pictures in the sky, and those pictures are the constellations."

Amelia Bedelia squinted her eyes and studied the stars above. She concentrated on drawing an imaginary line from one star to the next. She was making her own constellation, and she was going to name it Finally.

"Canis Finally"

117

It was super late when they got back to their cabin. "Now you are truly Polaris girls," said Peggy. "Sleep in tomorrow! We'll skip exercising, and I've arranged for us to have brunch instead of breakfast."

Amelia Bedelia put on her pajamas, brushed her teeth, and climbed into her bunk. She looked at her countdown calendar on the cabin wall and realized that she had only seven more days to go before her parents visited. The days were flying by. One last week to go, and then . . .

Chapter 11

"A Little Cricket Told Me"

The next week zoomed by. The weather had turned hot and humid. Dragonflies filled the air, and the crickets were chirping like crazy.

"It's too early to be so hot," said Peggy, glancing at her watch.

"I'm already sweating," said Alisha.

"Even my sweat is sweating," said Amy.

"Oh, *charmant*," said Annette.

"At least the lake will be warmer," said Amelia Bedelia.

"Hey, Amy, how hot is it?" asked Alice.

Amy wore a watch that told the time as well as the temperature. She pressed a button. "Time: eight eighteen a.m.," said the watch.

"And it's eighty-two degrees," said Peggy.

"Temperature: eighty-two degrees," said the watch.

The girls stared at Peggy.

"Okay, we give up," said Alice. "How did you know the temperature?"

Peggy told them her secret while they waited for Mrs. Evans and the morning announcements.

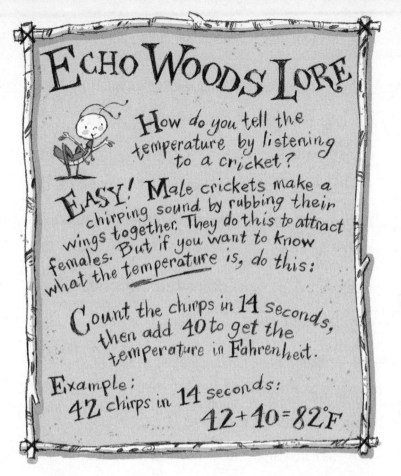

ECHO WOODS LORE

How do you tell the temperature by listening to a cricket?

EASY! Male crickets make a chirping sound by rubbing their wings together. They do this to attract females. But if you want to know what the temperature is, do this:

Count the chirps in 14 seconds, then add 40 to get the temperature in Fahrenheit.

Example:
42 chirps in 14 seconds:
42 + 40 = 82°F

At eight thirty sharp, Mrs. Evans arrived. "Wakey, wakey campers!" she said. "We are celebrating the halfway point of our summer with our traditional scavenger hunt. Your counselor has your marching orders! Be back by twelve thirty or be square. The cabin that finds the most, wins—and, remember, if you find the tenth thing on your list, you are the immediate champion. Break a leg! Today will be a scorcher, but don't get hot and bothered. If you start feeling queasy, see the nurse pronto!"

"Lots of luck, ladies," said Peggy, handing Alice the list of items. "You're on your own without me, but stick together. Like glue, please."

Alice read the list out loud. "An ice cube . . . a thermometer . . . a Popsicle stick . . ."

"Seriously? Everything makes me think about being hot," said Alisha.

"Let's think cool thoughts," said Amelia Bedelia. "Icy-cold ideas."

The Straight As waded through the shimmering heat and humidity.

"I'm on a silver sled and I'm sliding down a mountain," said Alice.

"Cool," said Annette, shutting her eyes as though she were imagining that.

"I'm making a snow angel," said Alice, doing jumping jacks.

"I'm making snow angels in my bathing suit," said Alisha.

A shiver ran through Amy. "*Brrrr!* I'm feeling frosty!"

Amelia Bedelia couldn't think of anything cool to say. But she loved how they sang a lot of songs at

Camp Echo Woods. Tilting her head back, Amelia Bedelia belted out a song that celebrated the cold.

"Good King Wenceslas looked out,
On the Feast of Stephen.
When the snow lay round about,
Deep and crisp and even."

As soon as they stopped laughing, the other girls joined in at the top of their lungs. They sang about cold and frosty weather. They sang about sleighs and snowmen and skating. Holding up her hand for silence, Alisha said, "Quiet, I'm taking the temperature." Fourteen seconds and forty-five chirps later, she

announced, "Eighty-five degrees."

All morning, the Polaris girls dragged themselves from one end of the camp to the other. Soon, it was almost time for the scavenger hunt to end. They paused at the big map of the camp, on their way back to the dining hall, and Alice took stock of what they'd found.

"Okay, we have the ice cube, a thermometer, a Popsicle stick, a piece of moss . . ."

"We shouldn't have gotten the ice cube first," said Annette, pouring water onto the ground.

"We're not doing so hot," said Alice.

"And we're getting hotter and hotter," said Amelia Bedelia, swaying a little bit.

"Uh-oh," said Alice. "Sit down before you fall down."

Amelia Bedelia sat in the shade. She leaned against the trash can painted with daisies. She closed her eyes and began counting chirps. Then she did the math. Eighty-eight degrees!

"What's the tenth thing on the list?" asked Annette. "Maybe we can still find that."

"A litterbug," said Alice. "Which is super weird."

Litterbug

Sweat was streaming down Amelia Bedelia's cheeks, almost as if she was crying. "Be cool, be cool," she whispered, wishing that snow lay round about, deep and crisp and even.

"Well, someone has it made in the shade!"

Amelia Bedelia looked up. Mrs. Evans was towering over her, with the camp nurse next to her.

"We got reports that you Polaris girls were delirious," said Mrs. Evans. "And singing about snowmen in ninety-degree heat."

"Eighty-eight degrees, actually," said Amelia Bedelia.

"I stand corrected," said Mrs. Evans.

"I sit sweating," said Amelia Bedelia. She stood up, but she was still wobbly.

"Feeling dizzy?" asked the nurse. "Try lowering your head."

Amelia Bedelia did. When she opened her eyes, she was looking at the world upside down. The first thing she saw was the trash can.

"Gotcha," said Amelia Bedelia. She went over to the trash can and turned it upside down. Litter spilled onto the ground.

"She's delirious!" said the nurse.

"Number ten. Litterbug," said Amelia Bedelia.

"Hats off to you, Amelia Bedelia," said Mrs. Evans. "No one, in all the years of Camp Echo Woods, has ever found it before, although your mother came close. You caught the litterbug!"

The Straight As gathered around the upside-down trash can. The daisies did not look like daisies anymore. They looked like a creepy-crawly spidery thing with yellow eyes and spiky hair.

"Hooray!" shouted Alice.

"Incroyable!" said Annette.

Just then, something furry and fast ran past the girls and dove into the pile of litter.

"Finally!" Amelia Bedelia shouted, grabbing her

collar and burying her face in Finally's soft fur.

"Why, welcome back," said Mrs. Evans, turning to greet Amelia Bedelia's parents. She gave Amelia Bedelia's mother a big welcome-home hug, then led everyone up to the dining hall.

Chapter 12

Sticks and Stones Won't Break This Bone

After lunch and an awesome scavenger hunt awards ceremony, Amelia Bedelia and the Polaris girls returned to their usual routine while Mrs. Evans took Amelia Bedelia's parents on a tour of the camp. They met up at the archery range to see Alisha shooting the last arrow of the day.

"Archery was always my favorite,"

said Amelia Bedelia's mother.

"And I recall that you were very good at it," said Mrs. Evans.

"Give it a go," said Peggy, offering Amelia Bedelia's mother a bow.

"Go ahead, Mom," said Amelia Bedelia.

Peggy pulled an arrow from her quiver for Amelia Bedelia's mother. Fitting the bowstring into the nock of the arrow, her mother planted her feet firmly on the ground, then drew the bowstring back

in one swift but steady motion. For the second or two that her mother held that pose, Amelia Bedelia gazed at her, wondering if she was really the goddess Artemis she'd studied about in school.

TWANNNNG! went the bowstring.

ZINNNNNNG! went the arrow.

THWACKKK! went the target.

There was a second of silence. Then "HOORAY!" went the Polaris girls.

"Bull's-eye!" shouted Alisha.

"Yay, Mom!" shouted Amelia Bedelia, glancing over her shoulder, looking for the bull.

"Nice job, sweetie," said Amelia Bedelia's father. "But I think I can top

Artemis Goddess of the Hunt

TWANNNNG! ZINNNNNNG! THWACK!

that." He was patting his pants pockets, searching for something. "I thought I had an apple to put on top of Amelia Bedelia's head."

Annette's eyes grew large. "Does he think he's William Tell?"

"Honey," said Amelia Bedelia's mother. "These girls may not realize you're kidding."

"In that case, I'll do what Robin Hood did in this situation," he said. "My arrow will split your arrow in half."

TWOUNNG! went his bowstring.

ZWANNNG! went the arrow.

KLATTTER! went the arrow after it

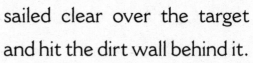 sailed clear over the target and hit the dirt wall behind it.

Woof! Woof! Woof!

"WOOF! WOOF! WOOF!" went Finally, chasing after the arrow.

"She thinks you're playing fetch," said Amelia Bedelia's mother.

"WOOF! WOOF! WOOF!" Finally kept barking at something behind the targets.

"Amelia Bedelia, please go get Finally," said her mother. "It's time to gather your things and head home."

"Home?" said Alice.

"Amelia Bedelia can't go home," said Annette.

"Well, it's up to Amelia Bedelia," said her mother, and she explained to the Polaris girls how they'd agreed to meet Amelia Bedelia halfway.

"No way!" said Alisha.

When Amelia Bedelia returned, she looked surprised, too. "Finally found something," she said.

"Not a skunk, I hope," said her father.

"Come look," said Amelia Bedelia.

Everyone followed Amelia Bedelia into the tall grass behind the row of targets, where Finally was still barking and racing back and forth in the weeds.

"What is it?" asked Mrs. Evans.

"I've never noticed anything out here

before," Peggy said in surprise.

"It's half buried, but it almost looks like a bone," said Amelia Bedelia's mother.

"It is a bone, or was a bone," said her father. "Probably a thighbone."

"What animal has a bone that big?" asked Amelia Bedelia, poking it with a stick.

"A dinosaur," said her father. "My guess is that this bone is a couple of hundred million years old."

"A fossil!" said Mrs. Evans. "Hot diggity!"

"Wow," said Amelia Bedelia. "A real-live fossil."

"Fossils are real-dead," said Amy.

"I have a friend at the university who specializes in dinosaurs," said Amelia Bedelia's mother. "I bet she'd love to come over and take a look at this."

"Call! Please!" said Mrs. Evans. "I'll be on the edge of my seat."

Then Mrs. Evans bent down and scratched Finally behind her ears. "As for you, my canine friend, you'll be getting a special treat for dinner tonight."

Annette began laughing. "Amelia Bedelia, your parents are truly *drôle*. What a silly joke!"

"What joke?" asked Amelia Bedelia.

"About you leaving us and going home," said Annette.

"I didn't want—"

Annette reached out and began tickling Amelia Bedelia under her chin.

"*Ha-ha-ha*," said Amelia Bedelia.

"See, you think it is ridiculous, too," said Annette.

"Very funny," said Alisha, tickling Amelia Bedelia under her arm.

"Make sure you stay away from her

neck," said Amelia Bedelia's father. "That always drives her crazy."

"Dad!" hollered Amelia Bedelia.

"Did you try behind her ears?" asked Amelia Bedelia's mother.

"Mom!" yelled Amelia Bedelia.

The rest of the Polaris girls had surrounded Amelia Bedelia, who was now wriggling on the ground. Amy was tickling her armpits. Alice was working

on spots behind both knees. Even Finally was helping by licking her face and neck.

"Mercy, mercy!" cried Amelia Bedelia, gasping for air between laughs.

Turning to Amelia Bedelia's parents, Annette said, "As you can hear, I have been teaching Amelia Bedelia how to speak French."

"Mercy," said Amelia Bedelia. "Mercy, mercy, mercy!"

"*Merci* means thank you," said Annette. Turning to Amelia Bedelia, she continued, "You are so welcome. We will take good care of you during the next four weeks."

"Lift on three!" said Alice. "One, two, THREE!"

Alice, Alisha, Annette, and Amy hoisted Amelia Bedelia into the air and onto their shoulders and carried her back to their cabin like ants carrying a prized

crumb back to their nest. She felt like the beloved beat-up teddy bear the girls had been fighting over when they first met.

Amelia Bedelia laughed and let her head flop back so she saw everything upside down. Her parents and Mrs. Evans and Peggy and even Finally were all upside down. She recognized them. She knew who they were. But like her summer, everything had been turned upside

down by coming to Camp Echo Woods.

Now, like her mother, Amelia Bedelia could not imagine her life without Camp Echo Woods. Amelia Bedelia might not be able to see where she was going, but one thing was certain—she was looking forward to her next four weeks of camp.

Two Ways to Say It ♥

By Amelia Bedelia

"Camp is a roller coaster."

"Both good and bad things happen at camp."

"The food isn't half bad."

"The food's actually pretty good!"

"That's neither here nor there."

"That doesn't really mean anything."

"What's wrong with this picture?"

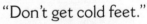

"Why doesn't this seem right?"

"Don't get cold feet."

"Don't lose your nerve and change your mind."

144

"Keep the wild animals at bay."

"Keep the wild animals away."

"Get it off the ground."

"Get it started."

"You are looking shipshape."

"You are looking neat and tidy."

"He was ahead of his time."

"His ideas were modern, even though he lived in the past."

"I am on the edge of my seat."

"I can't wait to see what happens next."

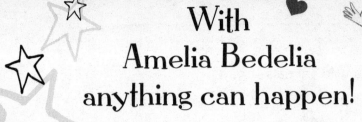

With
Amelia Bedelia
anything can happen!

The Amelia Bedelia ChapterBooks

Have you read them all?

#1

#2

#3

#4

How to make a French Braid

with Amelia Bedelia

C'est la vie!

1. Gather a big chunk of hair. Divide it into 3 parts.

2. Start a traditional braid by bringing the right strand over the center strand, then crossing the left strand over the center.

first

then

③ Now bring in new hair. Before crossing the next strand to center, add more hair from that side.

④ Continue adding hair in from each side, until it's all included in your braid.

⑤ When you get to the nape of your neck, continue with a traditional braid, and end with a hair tie.

VOILA!
c'est fini!!!

What Mrs. Evans says . . .

"Heavens to Murgatroyd, here we are for another summer at Echo Woods. Welcome back, ladies, and welcome to our five new campers. Now that your kit and caboodle is stowed, Counselor Peggy will show you the whole shebang. Just don't expect to be mollycoddled or live the life of Riley. Nothing namby-pamby lasts very long out here in the boondocks.

"Our cook is making grub that will stick to your ribs. We have a wonderful nurse, should anyone come down with the whim-whams, a case of the collywobbles, or just the heebie-jeebies. There won't be any flies in the ointment.

"About the only thing that bugs me is a litterbug. That's when I see red. Now you know how I feel, so we won't shilly-shally another second. Let's seize this summer. Onward!"

What Mrs. Evans actually means . . .

"Can you believe it? It's time for another summer at Echo Woods. Welcome back, ladies, and welcome to our five new campers. Now that you've unpacked, Counselor Peggy will show you where everything is and how everything works. You aren't at home, though, so don't expect any special treatment! You need to be tough and brave to live out here in the wilderness.

"Our cook is making food that is delicious and nutritious. We have a wonderful nurse, in case anyone gets scraped up or sunburned or stung by a bee or concerned about anything at all. But don't worry, everything will be just fine!

"About the only thing that bothers me here at camp is littering. That's when I get mad! Now that you know not to litter and to have fun, let's not waste any more time. Hooray for summer! Let's have a wonderful one!"